Toh's Saga

A Journey in Free Verse

By

Edward Eaton

A Verse Novella from
Dragonfly Publishing, Inc.

TOH'S SAGA
Verse Novella
Released in 2014

Paperback Edition
EAN 978-1-936381-95-1
ISBN 1-936381-95-8

Published in the United States of America by
Dragonfly Publishing, Inc.
Website: http://www.dragonflypubs.com

TABLE OF CONTENTS

Acknowledgements

I would like to thank the noted astronomer, Carl Sagan (1934-1996). This work is, to some degree, inspired by a passage I read in <u>Cosmos</u> some years ago: "I am skeptical about most of the extraterrestrial visions, [which] rely on forms of life we already know.... I do not think life anywhere else would look very much like a reptile, or an insect or a human—even with...minor cosmetic adjustments.... But if you pressed me, I could try to imagine something rather different." Chapter II, "One Voice in the Cosmic Fugue."

Dedication

As always, I would like to dedicate this work to my wife, Silviya, and my son, Christopher

Sine Quibus Non

Prologue

A spark of thought is
Hidden in cloud until it
Grows into a lightning bolt

I

IT has no name yet
It sees nothing within
Or without the emptiness

    It has no thoughts yet
Nothing no one joins it
Sees it loves it
Or
Knows its texture or touch

    It has no body

    It is still part of the other
Part of the

    WHOLE

II

EN is

    Riding the flow that is
Its home

    En floats
And wanders with its kind
Never knowing what is to come
Never caring what was

    En is

    Its many feelers reach out and
Search its kind for friend and foe
Reach past its own into beyond
To touch currents differing from
The one that carries it

    Many-feelered En is

    Large and awkward and bloated
It is powerful and its large
Gaseous body bumps and drifts
Through its kind taking in
Smaller ones that cannot flee
Hiding from the greater ones its feelers find
Avoiding being taken
Eating not eaten
Ruling never a slave
But to the WHOLE

    En is

En slips and glides through the stream
That flows with the current
Just below the ice

En is

Just one of many
Unknown
Just a part
It grows and feeds
It struggles and survives

En is

III

EN is

    Lonely En floats in the calm
As the whole waits
For a gentle push
A pool of warmth nestles them
All together

    En feels
At first it is an idea
Waiting to be conceived
Then it becomes many bubbles that
Drift through En's magnificent body
They flow back and forth
A thousand a hundred thousand small they
Tickle En

    One of many
One bubble of many
One bubble fights
And strives as it seeks without looking
A nesting place
IT latches on to En's strong skin

    And rests

    They are

En feels the bubble
The bubble inside
The other
The new
Form that feeds and rests
And grows
En feels IT
Growing

En waits
Not knowing what is to come
Not remembering its own birth
So long ago
So long ago

Could magnificent En
Vast-bodied En
Many-tentacled En have been
Have ever been so
Have ever been so small?
So small

Powerful En
Could powerful En
Who fought, who strove
Strove to command all within reach
Of its winding tendrils

Could so powerful En have been so
Inconsequential?
Trivial?
Could this
Insignificant
This nothing
Grow to rule
Similar domain?

Does En think this?
Does hulking En foresee decline?

En feels
En feels within, the tiny pressure
It is a new feeling
A new sensation
Neither welcomed nor abhorred

IT merely is

New to En
Old to all kinds
A pinprick that begins
To suck ITS fragile life from
En's greatness
A small spark that begins to burn
To consume
The other bubbling ITS that
Beat themselves against En
Against En's shell
And seek purchase

The many ITS which burst and make En grumble
The tiny one holds ITS own and
Keeps ITS grip
And feeds on the gasses En feeds on
And takes En's strength
En's formidable strength
For ITS own

    IT grows
En tries
En struggles and
Belches and tries what it can to vomit the small one
To no avail
The small one feeds and grows
Eating the others also inside
They cannot fight
Drawn as they are to the
Growing brilliance

    Soon IT is alone inside
The others gone
Surrendered
Absorbed

    En groans and fights
Is it fear En feels
Knowing the growing one
Will not go away?
Is it anger that En's
Solitude
Is no more?

    En reaches out with its tentacles
Many-tentacled En reaches out
And for strength and support
Its arms twisting and pulling
And dancing
Trying to hold onto the others
Trying to maintain its place in
The
WHOLE

    En
Shakes

    En
Quivers

En
Struggles

En
Fights

En knows it will
Lose
The one inside has grown too
Large the WHOLE knows
The others without know
And grab and snatch at
The weakened tentacles
Stealing them from the still
Raging En

En
Beset on all sides
—Inside and out—
Weakens
Bereft of its great strength
En shrinks away from the whole
And tries to hold its insides inside
Tries to remain whole
Tries to remain one

The small one eats En's strength
The small one grows
Soon IT pushes against En's side and
Splits En's flesh

Desperately pained En tries
En frantically tries to keep its side
Closed and the OTHER inside
En's whole being contracts and
Spins and quivers
Silent screams deafening the WHOLE
Silent screams rippling
Through the WHOLE

    The others sigh knowing what is to come
Grateful it has yet to happen to them
They flex their new arms
They reach out their newly taken tentacles
Pushing En from them

    The tear grows

    The still small being forces itself
From En and braves the warm liquid
Outside
Then with one great heaving
PUSH
IT pushes
Itself out
Is caught up in the current and

    Is

    Alone

    En is alone
Deflated
Small
En's few tentacles reach out
Barely-tentacled En reaches out
Searches
Sending giving the new one a
Gentle caress as they part

    En is
Small and weak
Alone among many
Fading into the rest
No longer master

IV

TOH
Toh is
Glorious it bursts
Forth
And leaves the wrinkling shell of
En
Behind

    Proud is Toh
Full of new life
Alone Master of its fate

    Toh is
Greeting each new sensation
With confused joy of
New birth

    Barely is Toh aware of
Diminished En
Toh floats and drifts away from
It dying-dead-forgotten-shriveled-fleeing parent
Forgotten in the first great
Flush of fresh awareness

    Toh is
One
Among many newborn
Naked in the midst of the WHOLE
One
Of many
Among many more
The newborn are
Shepherded
Gathered
Shepherded and gathered by the others
By the elder ones still strong and
Vibrant their
Many tendrils flex and push the
Newborn to the center of the
WHOLE
To the center
To safety and warmth and food

    A few
Some few of the newborn
Make not the safety of the center
Great tendrils snatch at them and
Pull them in
Absorbing them
Consuming them quietly and boldly
Taking them in to older ones who
Hunger for youth's vibrant energy

There is no struggle those
Unfortunate newborn can make

    Their pinprick lives are merely
Snuffed
Cut short

Many
Many of the newborn
Slip past
Slip past the snatching tentacles
End up in the safety of the center

Toh
Slips past
These snatching tentacles
Ends up among the other
Newborn
In the
Center

There are many
Many in the center
All young unaware of what
Is without

A few
Some few of the older young with
Their several tentacles
Leap forth and
Pounce on the newly arrived
Trying for one last safe meal
A last easy feeding
Before they are dragged away from safety
From the safety of
The nursery
Sent to take their places in the WHOLE
Sent out to be fully grown-not-young

Toh avoids
Toh eludes
These older young
Slipping by and joining the group
The mass-no-mass of newborns
Sliding past the outstretched tendrils
That tentatively reach out and
Move away as Toh is swept
Into the center

Toh is
One of many
It rests among the other
Newborn
In the center
In the center of the WHOLE
They drift along
Feeding

A few
Some few
Are small
Smaller than the others
Tiny
Little more than bubbles with the dimmest
Flicker of life inside
The least awareness
These few who slipped past the
Hungry elders the fierce and the strong
Are soon prey
Soon consumed
Soon eaten by
Those newborn that are
Larger
Hungrier
Stronger
They absorb the tiny ones
And grow

Toh feeds on these tiny ones
The tiny ones helplessly bump against it
They stick to its thin skin and then
Disappear inside
Toh is neither aware
Nor does it care
What pain these tiny ones may feel

Toh feeds
The tiny lives becoming part of its brighter one
The tiny ones becoming one with it

Toh grows
And feeds
And grows

Toh sweeps along in the
Center of the WHOLE
Dragged by an ever
Changing
Current
An ever-changing current
That moves the WHOLE
That carries the WHOLE
That is the WHOLE's

Home

World

Universe

    Snug in the center of the WHOLE
Toh drifts
Slipping against larger newborn
Which try to suck it in
To feed on it
But
Toh can slip away
They can feed on others not Toh
Not Toh

    They can not feed on Toh

    Toh survives

    Toh feeds

    Toh grows

V

WHAT of En?

Used
Spent
En drifts
Away from the center

There is the occasional flicker
An acknowledging touch
A recognition
Lord-no-master En
No longer reaches out and
Commands
But drifts

Weakened

Spent

Finished

En has borne Toh and is no longer needed
En has given
Given Toh to the WHOLE
Now is spent
Sent to drift along with others

So used

So spent

On the outskirts of the WHOLE
Where nearest friend in just within reach
Of outstretched tendril
Where all within reach are likewise spent
And now serve to protect the WHOLE

En has given a newborn
Now rests on the fringe
To give again to foreign enemy
To preserve the WHOLE
En's once greatness a mere
Shadow of a
Reflection of an
Idea of a
Memory

En

VI

TOH is

    Young

      It grows among the newborn
Lives and grows
A thousand nerves
A thousand million strands of hair-thin nerves
Branch and snake throughout the
Growing thickening-skinned orb that is
Toh
Grows and takes in more life and
Glows with health and strength

    Toh is

    Strong

      It rests-drifts-floats-swims in the center
The safest spot in the WHOLE
The hungriest spot
Furthest from danger
Furthest from foreign curiosity
Furthest from outside hunters
Furthest from food
But Toh perseveres
Toh manages
To feed and grow
In safety

Small Toh
Bigger and bigger it becomes
Caring not for concerns
Beyond its skin

Toh lives and feels within itself
The outside not but
Food
Threat

Toh is part but

Alone

The newborn do not romp and play
But nervously avoid fatal touch
They hide
As tendrils whip and flail
Through the nursery
Preying
On the lost
The weak

The helpless

A tentacle
Glides through the nursery
Glides snakelike through the nervous newborn
It brushes against Toh and
Sticks
To Toh's outer skin

Now Toh knows fear
Waits to be drawn
Away from the nursery
Waits to be consumed
Waits to be snuffed out

Toh uses the current
Toh uses the flow
And tries to break away to
Part from the tendril
That holds on to it

Twists

Turns

Do not dislodge the tendril

Gradually

Slowly

Toh rolls along the flat side of the tendril
That presses in
Its edge
Slicing into Toh's fragile
Shell
Minute drops of Toh's inner
Gas
Its lifeblood
Seep from Toh's wounds and flow

Away

Toh senses nearby others
Sense the preciousness
Nearby
They lash out with their tentacles
And snatch up the fresh food
But miss wounded
Toh
Moves along the tendril which
Waves and yaws
And quivers

Finally

Finally Toh reaches an end
Toh comes to the end of the tendril
To find

Emptiness

No thing stronger or
Dangerous
Awaits Toh at the end
Just an end
That flops in the stream

The sharp tip is drawn to
Toh
Presses against it

Somehow Toh knows
Toh instinctively knows
That this tendril is for Toh
No other lies at the other end
Waiting to take Toh in
This tendril is alone
Unclaimed
Not part of an other

Why?

Why is this tendril

Alone?

Alone unclaimed
Wandering aimlessly with the current
In the middle of the whole
Untaken?

Perhaps it has drifted
Many lifetimes
Along the current
Finally to be washed into
The community
Driven into the middle of the WHOLE
Driven by fate to be with Toh
To become part of Toh

Perhaps it was lost
Disgorged by some dying elder?
Could it even have come from En?
Once-great En unknowingly sending
Offspring Toh its first limb
A birthday present from absent parent

Or was it lost in some great
Fight
Strife
As others fought for
Precious fare?

Whatever else may be
Toh knows
Toh knows this is for Toh
The sharp edge presses against Toh's
Skin
Pushing in
Piercing

The pain is great

Great is the pain that races through
Toh's nerves
The end enters Toh letting out Toh's
Precious fluid
Toh
Contracts
Holds the skin together forcing the
Tendril away
The tendril forced away
Flaps in the current
Flaps and waves and searches for Toh

Tentatively
The tendril finds Toh
Once again
Finds Toh and presses its sharp point
Its sharp end
Against the nervous flesh
Against the innocent flesh
Pressing into unblemished Toh

One great flash of
Pain
Then Toh's skin grips
Wraps itself around
The tendril
And holds fast

They are together now

Toh and tendril

Master and slave

Body and limb

VII

TOH rests
Worn by its deflowering
Exhausted by the change

    For a time rests
Toh
Tentatively tests its new limb

    New Sensations flow through
Toh
Basks in new fou—

    Something
Something is
Some thing is
Wrong
Toh cannot control the tendril
As it should

    Toh tugs
It pulls
But cannot control the limb

    New to the limb
Toh does not know how it should
Feel
But knows it is
Wrong

    Toh feels
The tendril pull against it
Jerk and snap as if
Trying to get away

Toh knows

Toh realizes

Toh feels

Great fear

Toh is not alone on this
Tendril
Toh's tentacle
Toh's limb
Is
Claimed
By an Other

Rare is it
When tendril
Claimed
By two newborn
Becomes focus of a
Mighty fight

Waves screaming of strife
Tell the WHOLE the story
That Toh lives through

Toh tugs the tentacle
Tentatively
The Other jerks back
Soon the two are orbiting
Each other
In mute fury
They spin and twirl

They brush against smaller newborn
Ignoring ready food as they
Hold on to precious limb

They swing by elders
Waiting
Expecting to feed
On the loser's remains
And greet the winner into the
Community

The two careen about the
Nursery

Slashing

Whipping the tendril
Laying waste to unfortunate babes
Who stray into the battleground
Leaving trails of life fluid that
Spray across the center

Soon Toh is weary
Rests
Drifts toward the hungry Other

There is an expectation
A waiting
For an
End

It is not only
Toh
That waits for a
Finish
An end

It is not only
Toh
That waits for a
Finish

An electricity

A feeling

Spreads through the area
Realizing
Knowing
That a change is
Coming

Toh drifts
Gradually moving
For the Other at the
Far end

Many lifetimes drifts
Toh
The Other seemingly
Teasing its
Prey
Resting
Preparing
To devour
To end
Toh

Tension
Rips through the nursery
Many tentacles dance and flit
Awaiting the outcome
Snatching bits of lifeblood
That float near the
Battleground
Hovering to welcome the
Victor

To embrace the new
Sibling

Toh drifts
Along the flat of the great
Limb

Finally
At last
Toh meets the
Foe

There is no
Sudden
Victory

There is no
Swift

Dénouement

There is no
Bloody

Finale

Toh's foe is
Worn
Beaten
Bloody

The two orbs
Press
Against one another

Rippling and groaning they
Push

The two are
Frozen in their
Embrace
And then become
One

   The larger devouring the smaller
The weaker joining its
Spark of life to the
Stronger
And the greater
Growing
With new power and blood

   Toh is

   Alive

   Victor

   There are Heroes
Conquerors
Warriors
In a thousand lifetimes
From a thousand million lifetimes
On an ever growing number of worlds
Subject to countless tales
Legends
Of great deeds

   Toh knows nothing of these
Its mighty battle
Forgotten by the whole
As soon as it is over
But it was a great deed
For now Toh
Is undisputed
A power in the nursery
Possessor of a great limb
Its victory no less
Heroic
Than Hector's futile stand
'Gainst the petty divine

Exhausted
Toh rests
Ignoring the many tendrils that
Lap up its mighty foe's remains

Toh
Lazes
The precious limb drifting behind
Toh

A sign

A warning

A part of

Toh

Is

Part of the
WHOLE

Toh
Awakens to the dawn of its new
Maturity
Toh stretches out the limb
Reaches out with the tendril
As if in a yawn
Reaches out to touch
To explore
Toh's home
Reaches out a thousand times further than
Toh could have before

Toh
Brushes the tentacle
Along the limbs of others
A brief hello
Acknowledgement
Then moving on

Toh catches bits of food that
Float along the current
Drawing them along the tentacle
Absorbing them
Growing stronger

Newborn bump into Toh
To be pushed away
Firmly
Toh is growing
Is no longer a callow
Newborn
The limb proclaims identity
Outside the nursery
Not yet a full adult

Toh grows
Toh eats
Toh strengthens
Toh drifts from the center
Guided by the others
Becoming a full part of the WHOLE

The WHOLE

Adjusts

Grows

Strengthens

VIII

TOH is
Part of the Whole
One of Many

Many thousands
Hundreds of thousands
Thousands of millions
Perhaps

There is no one
No one to count the
Number of
Orbs
That drift along the current

The current that flows
Beneath a sky of ice

A frigid home for the many
Creatures
Beings
Who live on this

Forgotten
World
That orbits an
Unknown sun
In the corner of
Nowhere

No
Great
Cities
Dot the
Icescape

No
Great
Civilizations
Grow and
Thrive and
Explore this
World

No
Great
Poets
Sing songs of the
Land or of the
Gods and
Heroes

The world is merely a block of
Ice

A giant snowball
Hurled by some
Eternal hand and
Left to
Fly
Untended

A solid center
Layers of liquid
Capped by solid
Ice

The surface is

Empty

Unwelcoming
An infinite waste of
Storms and drifts and
Whirling snow
Enough to frighten even the most
Resolute explorer should
One
Brave the
Rocks the
Countless small
Moons and
Clouds of
Dust that cloak this
Abominable Eden

But below
Below the granite clouds
Beneath the malshapen hideous ice is
Fluid

Fluid
Floes
In tiny creeks
Vast oceans
Mighty cataracts
Serene pools

And in this juice
Teems
Life

Small communities
Large colonies
Intrepid loners
Make the fluid
Home

Great leviathans
Wander
Below the ice
Mashing and gnawing
Their lives
Recklessly from food to
Food

Small
Microscopic
Families
Scurry and skimmer
Along the edges of the
Flow

Together
Apart
Hunting
Hiding
Helping
Fighting
Eating
Surviving
Unseen and
Seeing they
Live their lives
Quietly secluded from the
Cosmos

Toh's Whole
Lives
Here
Master of many
Prey for some
It has its
Place in the flow
In the current
Beneath the ice
Above the molten core

The Whole is made up of
Many
Uncounted
Uncountable
Many

    The Whole protects the
Newborn
The many newborn in their
Nurseries
Allowing them to feed on
What little nourishment
Passes through the
Interstices
In the latticework of
Tentacles that is
The amount of the Whole

    The nurseries though are
Small sedate
Pools

    But from the nurseries
Burst
Strong
Vibrant
Youths
Who dance and
Wrestle in a
Cloud of arms

    From the Great Ones they
Snatch precious limbs
And reach out and
Know their home
Their domain

Each tentacle adds to the
WHOLE
Each limb increases the
Total
Each limb speaks to the
Others
Each limb tells the story of its
Reach
Each fragile limb cries out into the
Dark Current
Warning strangers of the
Great Size of the
Awesome Fury of the
WHOLE

The great masters assume their places and
Rule beyond the
Callow youths
Their mighty limbs stretch forth from
Their massive bodies
Reach out beyond the present of the
Whole and
Into the
Future ahead and the
Past behind

The mighty many-tentacled masters
Strut in sublime solitude
Flexing
Waving
Their limbs

They are the strength of the
WHOLE
Their silent cries
Their fierce demeanor
The shell that keeps the
WHOLE
One

They toughen youths
By surrendering their
Tendrils
And move
Allowing the
WHOLE
To grow
They part with their strength
To make the
WHOLE
Stronger

Beyond the mighty
Are the
Old the
Feeble the
Wasted

There is En
Weakened through labor
Once great
Once
Mighty
Now
Past prime
Past youth
Past joining in the
Collective as
Equal partner

Those like En
Suffer the end of usefulness as
Shield to the
Whole

    They warn the mighty of
Danger and
Cast off to feed
Destruction and
Death and
Slow the
Invading
Chaos
Without

    Thus ends
En

    En was

    En
Is
Not

    Taken
By a hungry hunter

    Crushed against the
Ice
Above or a
Rock
Below

    Swept away by a
Different
Indifferent
Current

    To be lost

Trampled by the
WHOLE
Gathered
Crumped
Clumped
As the colony drips through a
Narrow
Bottleneck and
Spat out the other
Side

Perhaps En simply drifted away
Unable to keep up
Unable to be
Unwilling to accept
Diminished place
No longer caring to keep up

Those like En
Simply disappear
Gone
Are no longer
Part of the
WHOLE
Wanted
No longer

Their places taken
By others
Weak
Old
Newborn
Wasted
Sickly
Useless
Make room for the
Rest
Sacrificed to preserve the
Strong

The colony

The collective

The WHOLE

IX

TOH is
Mighty Toh
Many-feelered Toh
Has place in the Whole
Among the mighty masters

    Toh

    Stands
Out
Great and
Powerful

    Toh's many
Tendrils
Toh's arms
Stretch out and
Command
Vastness

    Little food gets past
Toh's tentacles
Which snatch up all
That come within
Reach and
Leave the rest to
Pine and
Groak
And shrivel

Toh also adds
Many newborn so
Unfortunate as to
Crawl
Into its
Reach on their
Journey to the nurseries
They are rolled in and
Become part of Toh's
Hulking
Murfled
Body

Sad lost newborn
Never to feel freedom but
To become part of
Mighty Toh
Whose limbs reach out
Many thousand times the length and width of
Toh's bulging sack
Reaching out through the emptiness

A finite reach that
Marks the boundaries of
Toh's
Limits

The mighty beyond Toh
Cringe at a touch

The inner youth
Give wide berth

The old and weak
Shrink as Toh
Picks away at their rotting dying sacks
Adding to itself

Toh was once a
Youth
Fresh from the crop of
Newborns

Toh once feared the
Mighty

But Toh
Young Toh
Hungry Toh
Was
Cunning

Toh sought out the
Embryc freshly born and
Snatched them as they
Carelessly thought they were
Close to the safety of the nursery

Toh spun
And drifted throughout
The Whole
And
Hunted
Those weak and torn by
Labor

Toh snatched at
Tentacles
Lost and alone or
Claimed by the weak
Toh took them to
Itself

Toh hoarded precious
Food

Toh
Attacked those weary from
Battle

Toh became
Mighty and
Strong

Toh hungered
Toh ate
Toh sought power over
Self

From time to time
A strong youth
Indicated a readiness
To enter the ranks of the
Mighty
This youth has survived the
Perilous journey from
Womb to
Nursery
Has fended self against
Other newborn
Struggling for nourishment
Has found limb before being
Pushed into the flow as
Fodder
Has taken limb and learned to
Feed and
Fight and
Finally
Flee the nursery and join the
Ranks of the young toughs
Bent on becoming stronger
Older
Surviving

From time to time
Such a youth will
Snake out its few tentacles
As if to speak to the mighty
To make it known said youth
Is ready to join their order

When the mighty feel themselves
In the touch of this
Brave one
They surrender some precious
Limbs
To the new strength
In welcome

This is the
Way
It has been
This is the
Way
It is
This is the
Way
It will be

En did it
The Ens before En
For they too had
Begged for
Acceptance and
Been given

As once did
Toh

For the
Strength the
Safety of the
Whole
Is volume
And volume is the
Number of the
Mighty and their
Far reach

The youth takes a few
Limbs and
Stretches out

The Mighty make way

The Mighty suffer
Diminishment
The WHOLE
Increases

As it has
So shall it
Be

But Toh
Hungers

Toh is
Selfish

Toh slaps away the gentle tug
Pushing the youth away

Go
Take from another

The silly youth
Tentatively
Tugs again

Toh's tendrils shoot out
Piercing the bold thief
Which backs away

Toh laps up the
Bubbles left behind

Leave
Be gone
Toh's domain is
Toh's
Alone

There is a stillness in the
WHOLE
Of shock and then
Of Anger

The Mighty must give to be stronger

The Mighty crowd Toh and
Gently push the youth ahead

Toh flails
Slicing and
Stabbing
Protecting its tendrils

The Mighty slap and
Spin and
Flail at Toh

Give to
Increase!
Give to the
WHOLE!

The Mighty
Pick and
Prick and
Prod and
Pull and
Push
But Toh
Will not surrender
Tendril one

They beat and
Slap

Voiceless screams
Disturb the flow

Toh spins and
Rolls and
Weaves and
Will not surrender
Tendril one
To these furies of the
WHOLE

Toh
Waits

Toh
Drifts

Waits for renewed attack

Toh waits

Toh reaches out
One tendril and spins

No thieves lurk to the side

Toh reaches out
One tendril and rolls

No thieves
Above or below

Toh reaches out
All limbs
Stretches out
None gone
Toh is whole
Toh is mighty
Toh is master

Toh is...

Toh reaches out
All limbs
Forcing them out
To the limit
Straining
Beyond the limit

Toh waves and feels for
Neighboring touch
Toh flails
Searching for
Neighboring orb

Toh finds
Nothing

    For as Toh lay and waited
In many-tentacled armor
The Whole drifted by
The Whole moved on
The Whole shifted and adjusted

    Leaving

    Toh

    Alone

X

TOH is
Alone

    Cast out

    Abandoned by the
WHOLE

    Toh put
Self
Above the WHOLE
The community and
Now is no longer a
Part
No longer among the
Mighty

    There is
None
Within reach

    Disgusted by Toh's
Hunger
By Toh's
Refusal to give
The WHOLE has
Moved on
Adjusted

    Forgotten

Toh is no more
Toh is forgotten
Toh is
Alone

Toh stretches out

Nothing

Toh spins

Nothing

As far as Toh can
Reach
As far as Toh can
Feel
Is
Empty
Void
Barren
Bereft

Toh flails
Waves
To
No one

Blindly
Toh stumbles along the
Current
Desperately trying to
Touch

Anything

Something

Familiar

The pressure of the
Current
Increases

Toh brushes solid rock
Below

To the sides
Toh finds
Solid

The flow is being
Crushed into a
Bottleneck

Toh reaches up to
Pull away from the
Growing speed
The thickness

Toh reaches up and burns its tentacles
Against the hot ice
Above
Tentacles scorched
And withered by the
Heat

Toh wraps its
Tendrils around itself
And allows the flow to
Push it into the narrows
Ahead

Massive Toh
Sticks

Massive Toh
Scrapes against the
Jagged rocks the
Fiery ice

The pressure behind
Forces
Drags
Toh Forward

Toh bleeds and
Writhes
Inching along the cutting
Shards

Then
By the flow that
Builds and gathers behind
Toh's great bulk
Toh is shot forward
Thrust
Flung into the thinner
Beyond

Toh spins
And tumbles out of control
Out of reckoning and
Finally comes to
Rest

Tendrils ripped from Toh's
Body
Spiral and Twirl about
Some
Many
Eluding its
Desperate grabs

Bubbles or vital
Blood fluid
Drift by

Some gathered hungrily and
Weakly and
Re-swallowed
Re-consumed

Toh waits
While torn skin
Heals into rough
Coarsened scars

Toh waits
And feels the vastly
Powerful emptiness
In this new
Unknown
Fresh world
Below the ice

Toh flexes its
Many tendrils
Tenderly feeling
The area
Knowing
Masterdom and
Solitude and

Independence

Finally
Gently and tentatively
Toh reaches out its
Long limbs and finds
The stream that rushes
By Toh's foodless sanctuary

The tendrils cup and
Allow the stream to pull
Toh up and along

   Silently Toh flows
Past
Whole worlds
Just beyond reach
Unaware of them
Ignorant of the sublime and
Profane
Edens and
Hells

   Toh grabs what little
Food there is
Eagerly adding to the shrinking
Sack that was once so
Magnificently fat and full

   Long Toh flows and bounces
From stream to flow
Scrabbling out of doldrums
And around mountains of
Rock and ice that
Mar the
Sameness of the flow

   In time
Toh even loses the flow
Leaving the weakening stream
Far away
Drifting in a great desert
Pool

   Toh waits

   No new streams are there
To drag Toh to fresh feeding grounds

No errant flows bring Toh
Precious sustenance

Toh waits and
Shrinks and
Shrivels and
Hungers and
Starves

Toh hungers not only for food
But also for the reassuring touch of
Kindred kind

Toh is
Lonely

Toh has forgotten the WHOLE
But recalls that once its
Mightiness was known
And powerful

Toh waits
Not knowing of Death's gentle
Seduction
But aware that soon Toh will
Cast itself out
Shall spit out
The ravenous tendrils
It can no longer care for
And the wasted
Husk of Toh will soon
Drift away into the
Unfeeling unknown of
Nowhere
Nowhen
Ever other gone

Toh waits with
Long tentacles hanging
Weakly

No longer do they
Search for food
No longer do they
Wait against hope
For fresh succor
They dangle helpless and
Tired and
Wave in the gentle tidal flow
Of back and forth
Rocking Toh

Something brushes against
Toh's tentacles
Rubbing
Resting
Dying

Toh is alert once more
Attentive and
Afraid

Tentatively
Toh stretches out in
Greeting

Expecting feelers
Tentacles from another lost one
Toh is greeted by

An OTHER

A Different

A Solid with a sleek
Thickery skin

The Solid nuzzles up to
Toh

It shows no
Fear to once-mighty Toh
Nor does is show
Respect

It merely swims into
The forest of limbs
Cold it allows the
Tendrils to wrap around and
Protect it from the
Swirling freezing liquid

Toh wraps its
Many arms about the
Solid and
Feels its gratitude
Thanking the fellow
Lost
Unloved
Unwanted

They float
These two in the never moving
Ever flowing
Virgin pool
Caressing and holding each other
No longer alone
No
Longer
Alone

At peace they drift
Blindly following the gentle
Current that rocks them
Calmly to restful
Sleep called
The death
They await and revere

Toh grips the Solid in an
Embrace
Carefully latching tentacles onto the
Rock beneath

Let them stay where they are
Toh thinks
Stay
Standing still so the dark emptiness
Can catch up all the quicker

The Solid squirms in Toh's
Gentle hug

Toh rocks them softly

The Solid struggles
Seems to say something

Wearily
Toh alerts its senses and waits to know

"Food"
The tired and muddled thought comes to Toh

"Food"

The thoughts rush clearly to mind

Not knowing why
But knowing to
Toh guides The Solid to the rock

The Solid latches onto the rock and
Will not move though
Toh tries with exhausted strength
The Solid will not move from the
Rock breast it suckles

Toh feels The Solid
Feels the great maw sucking the craggy rock
Feels the hard plates of scales that cover The Solid
A large round deflated Different that
Is alien to Toh

Toh gives the feeding Different a
Gentle stroke and begins to let go
This feast is no place for the starving hungry

A ripple glides across the surface of The Solid
Perhaps it is merely a farewell
Toh thinks

Then

Then

Then Toh feels a
Near forgotten feeling

Sensation

Surge

That fills with glowing
Toh's weakened body

A tiny prickling impression
The flows and
Grows and
Seeps along the withered
Tentacles the
Tired
Dying
Tendrils

Toh shudders and
Allows the food to
Enter to
Fill to
Revive

Toh feeds
Feeds off The Solid
Which feeds off the rock

Soon
All too soon
The Solid has suckled the
Rock
Dry
Reluctantly it releases the
Stony surface

Toh and the Solid
Entwined
Joined
Mated

In a twirling silent dance in the dark fluid
Catch the flow
They move along the
Current
Toh dragging it tendrils
Along the bottom in
Search of rocks in
Search of food

XI

TOH is

    Riding the flow that is
Its home

    Toh floats
And wanders with The Solid
The Droog
Remembering the loneliness
Hating it

    Toh is

    Its many feelers reach out and
Search for food

    Many-feelered Toh is

    Sleek and strong
It is powerful and its large
Gaseous body moves along the flow with
Purpose

    Toh is

    It slips and glides through the stream
That flows with the current
Just above the bed

    Toh is

Just one
One of two
Together
They grow and feed
They struggle and survive

They are

They are
Together

XII

TOH feels
At first it is an
Idea
Waiting to be conceived
Then it becomes many bubbles that
Drift through Toh's magnificent body
They flow back and forth
A thousand a hundred thousand small they
Tickle Toh

    Toh feels the bubbles
The bubbles inside
The others
The new
Forms that feed and rest
And grow
Toh feels them
Growing

    Toh waits
Knowing what is to come
Remembering its own birth

    So long ago

    So long ago

Epilogue

THE largest clouds burst
Forth great torrents rain then
Remain but a wisp

Author

Edward Eaton is the award-winning author of the young adult fantasy time-travel series *Rosi's Doors*, which includes <u>Rosi's Castle</u>, <u>Rosi's Time</u>, and <u>Rosi's Company</u>. He is also the author of the plays <u>Elizabeth Bathory</u>, <u>Hector and Achilles</u>, and <u>Orpheus and Eurydice</u>. He has been a newspaper columnist, a theatre critic, and a sometime scholar. He has studied taught at several colleges and universities in the States and overseas. He holds a PhD in Theatre History and Literature, and works frequently as a stage director and fight choreographer. In addition to his creative and academic pursuits, Ted is an avid SCUBA diver and skier. He lives and works in Boston, Massachusetts, with his wife Silviya, a hospital administrator, and his son Christopher.

* * * * *

www.ingramcontent.com/pod-product-compliance
Lightning Source LLC
Chambersburg PA
CBHW022050170626

46808CB00003B/1431